Princess Delphina's School

Oceana's House

Emerald's Dad's House

Emerald's School

Palace

For vampires, fairies, humans,
and MERMAIDS everywhere!
And for Bonnie Ocèa.

Illustrated by Mike Love,
based on original artwork by Harriet Muncaster

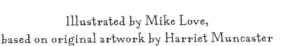

OXFORD
UNIVERSITY PRESS

Great Clarendon Street, Oxford OX2 6DP
Oxford University Press is a department of the University of Oxford.
It furthers the University's objective of excellence in research, scholarship,
and education by publishing worldwide. Oxford is a registered trade mark
of Oxford University Press in the UK and in certain other countries

First published in 2023
First published in paperback 2023

British Library Cataloguing in Publication Data

Data available

ISBN: 978-0-19-278873-3

1 3 5 7 9 10 8 6 4 2

Printed in China

Paper used in the production of this book is a natural,
recyclable product made from wood grown in sustainable forests.
The manufacturing process conforms to the environmental
regulations of the country of origin.

EMERALD

and the Ocean Parade

Harriet Muncaster

OXFORD
UNIVERSITY PRESS

Chapter ONE

TRRRRINGGGG went my clamshell alarm clock.

I sat up in bed feeling confused for a moment before I remembered where I was— in my bedroom in the royal palace! A few months ago, my mum and King Auster got married, which I suppose makes *me* a princess. I have two houses because I spend half my time at the palace and half with my dad, who lives in a small pearly pink house on the other side of Scallop City. I was still getting used to living in two different places and I was still getting used to being a princess. I didn't feel like one at all yet. I don't look anything like my graceful stepsister, Delphina. My hair is all spiky and wild (which is exactly how I like it) and I have a wriggly little octopus for a pet!

I slipped out of bed, uncurling my tail. Tiny bubbles danced in the water.

'Come on, Inkibelle!' I said to my pet

octopus, who was still snoozing soundly
on my sea-sponge pillow. 'Time to get up
for school!'

Inkibelle does not like getting up
for school.

I poked her but she only curled
up tighter, so I left her snoozing while
I swam out of my bedroom and down the
shell-studded corridor to the bathroom.
On my way, I bumped into Delphina.

'Emerald,' she cried.
'Good morning!' Then she
stretched her arms out
wide and I knew she
was coming in for a
hug. Delphina is a very
affectionate mermaid.
I found her a tiny bit
annoying when I first
moved in to the palace
a few months ago, but

I am getting used to her now.

'I'll race you to breakfast!' she cried, and then swished away in a flurry of bubbles.

'You're late!' said Mum when I finally made it down to the grand dining room, with Inkibelle swimming along behind me.

'Sorry!' I said. 'Inkibelle just didn't want to get up this morning!'

Inkibelle poked me crossly with one of her tentacles and pouted.

'Well it's *true*!' I said as I sat down next to Delphina, who was already tucking in to some sea-crunch cereal.

I pulled a slice of mermaid toast towards me and spread it thickly with pale green seaweed butter.

'We've been talking about the Ocean Parade!' said Delphina excitedly. 'I can't wait!'

Immediately I felt my insides fizz with excitement. I *love* the Ocean Parade! It happens every year to celebrate the new summer sea season arriving and I've been to it since I was a tiny mermaid. There's lots of delicious food, music and dancing, and everyone dresses up. Dressing up is my favourite part! A stream of pretty floats parade through the streets of Scallop City, including the royal carriage.

Last year I went to the parade with my school friends and it was the best day ever! We dressed up in all our spangles and sparkles, ate crispy-kelp and sea-flower floss and danced to music as the floats paraded by. I smiled as I remembered all the fun we'd had.

'I can't wait either!' I said.

Delphina grinned happily at me. 'What kind of headdress will you wear, Emerald?'

'Well, last year me and my friends bought sea-flower crowns from a stall and . . .'

'I mean which *royal* headdress will you choose!' said Delphina. 'You'll be in the carriage with the royal family this year, remember? It's tradition for us all to wear big fancy headdresses!'

I frowned and looked at Mum and Auster but they both just smiled and nodded.

'Your first parade in the royal carriage!' said Mum. 'Won't that be exciting!'

'Um . . .' I said. It hadn't occurred to me that I would have to ride in the royal carriage during the parade, but I supposed that I would have to, now I was a mermaid *princess*.

It was taking some getting used to.

'But the royal carriage rides through the centre of Scallop City and then ends up back at the palace,' I said. 'We won't have time to join in any of the fun!'

'There will be a special party back here at the palace,' smiled Auster. 'With very fancy food!'

I thought back to the crispy-kelp and sea-flower floss I had bought from a stall last year. I doubted there would be anything like that served at the palace. I don't think I'm really cut out to be a *proper* princess, I thought despondently.

I didn't look like one.

I didn't *eat* like one.

And I definitely didn't *feel* like one!

'Do I *have* to go in the royal carriage?' I asked. 'I'd much rather hang out with my school friends.'

Delphina's face fell and Auster looked a bit disappointed.

'I *mean*,' I said hurriedly. 'I don't think anyone will want to see *me* in the carriage.'

'Of course they will!' said Auster. 'You're a mermaid princess now! You absolutely have to be there.'

'You do,' agreed Mum firmly.

I sighed, putting my piece of toast back onto my plate. Suddenly I didn't really feel very hungry. The thought of not being able to go to the Ocean Parade with my friends was not a nice feeling. And the thought of having to sit in the royal carriage and be on show to everyone in the kingdom was even worse! I was nothing like Delphina. She looks and acts like a proper princess. I'm just . . . *me*.

'There's a headdress fitting this afternoon after school,' said Auster. 'It'll be fun, I promise.'

I nodded glumly and Mum tried to reassure me with an encouraging glance.

'Don't worry, Emerald,' she said.

14

'We'll find a headdress you really like.'

I gave her a watery smile.

'Maybe,' I said, doubtfully.

Chapter TWO

Delphina and I left the palace and swam
to school, with Inkibelle swishing along
behind us. Delphina doesn't have a special
pet but she does have a magical merteddy
bear! (A vampire-fairy called Isadora
Moon magicked it alive for her when she
was visiting our underwater kingdom!)
Delphina's merteddy goes everywhere

16

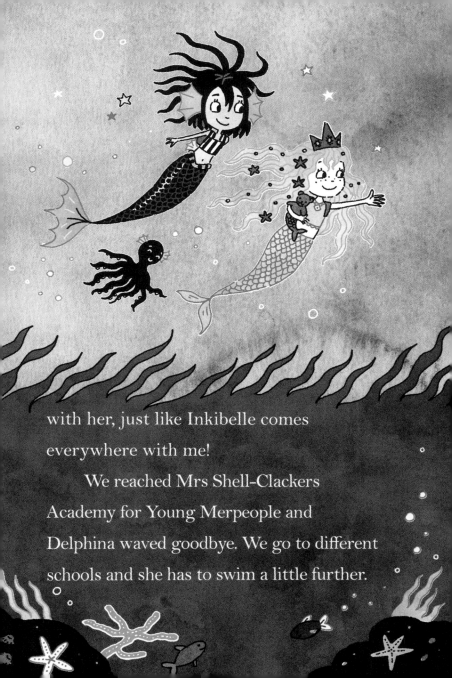

with her, just like Inkibelle comes everywhere with me!

We reached Mrs Shell-Clackers Academy for Young Merpeople and Delphina waved goodbye. We go to different schools and she has to swim a little further.

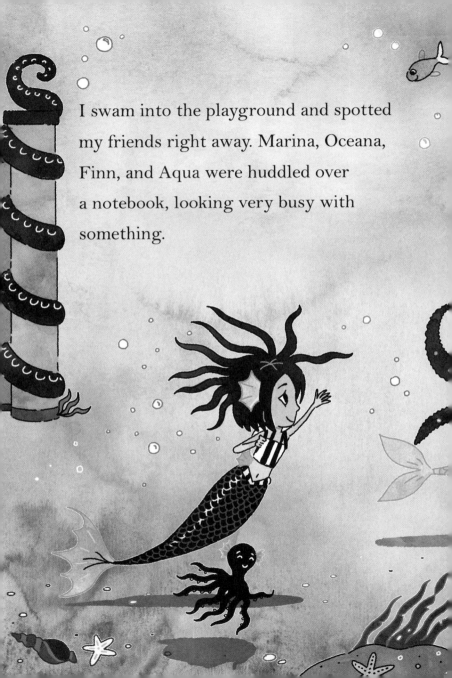

I swam into the playground and spotted
my friends right away. Marina, Oceana,
Finn, and Aqua were huddled over
a notebook, looking very busy with
something.

'Hi, Emerald!' said Marina, looking up. 'We're just designing our outfits for the Ocean Parade. Look, here's mine!'

She held the notebook out towards me and I stared at the page, impressed.

Marina had designed a beautiful top
with swathes of floaty material that would
swirl behind her in the water. She was
going to wear lots of pearl necklaces and
stick pearl beads all the way up and down
her arms too.

'Oh!' I breathed. 'It's so *you!*'

'That's what I said!' Oceana smiled.

I couldn't help but feel a tiny bit
jealous. I wished I could wear exactly
what I wanted to the Ocean Parade. But
unlike my friends, I was going to have to
wear a stupid old headdress and sit in the
royal carriage!

'Hey, let's design your outfit,
Emerald!' said Oceana. 'I expect you'll
want something a bit more edgy with lots
of sparkly dark greens in it.'

'I *would,*' I said. 'Except I'm sure
I won't be allowed to dress how I usually
do. I have to sit in the royal carriage this
year and wear a special royal headdress!'

'Really?' Marina sounded excited and a little bit disappointed, all at once.

'I thought you were coming to the parade with us,' said Finn.

'I thought I was,' I huffed.

'Don't you want to sit in the royal carriage?' asked Aqua. 'I think it sounds like fun.'

'I doubt it,' I said miserably. 'I'll probably do something un-princess-like and everyone will laugh.'

'You really *are* the most unlikely mermaid to become a princess!' Marina smiled.

A bolt of worry zinged through me.

22

'*That* is what I'm worried about!' I
replied. 'I don't feel like a princess at all!'

Marina put her arm around me.

'Don't worry, Emerald, you'll be
great! And we'll all make sure to wave at
you as you go past!'

'We'll feel *proud* to see our
friend in the royal carriage!'
added Aqua.

'Thanks,' I replied,
blushing and hiding my
face under my spiky
mop of black hair. My
friends always know
what to say to make me
feel better.

24

At the end of the day, Oceana asked if I wanted to go over to her house.

'The others are coming too,' she said. 'We're going to play catch the bubble!'

'Count me in,' I replied.

Catch the bubble is a special merpeople game where you have to race each other through the water after a silvery, magic bubble. It's very tricksy! The first one to catch the bubble is the winner. I felt excited as I packed away my things and swung my schoolbag over my shoulder, following Oceana, Marina, Finn, and Aqua into the playground. When I got outside, I was surprised to find my mum waiting for me. She never usually comes to pick me up from school.

'What are you doing here?' I asked.

'Don't you remember?' she said. 'We've got our headdress fitting.'

'Do I *have* to go?' I asked. 'I *really* want to go over to Oceana's and play catch the bubble!'

'Yes, Emerald, you do,' replied Mum. 'It's all booked in at Madame Cowrie's!'

'Oh,' I said again. I looked at my friends and shrugged.

'We can play catch the bubble another time,' said Marina.

'We'll see you tomorrow, Emerald!' said Finn.

I watched wistfully as my friends swam away together, chatting and laughing.

Without *me*.

It wasn't busy at Madame Cowrie's shop that afternoon because the whole place had been cordoned off especially for our visit.

We swam through the doors, into the posh boutique.

'Emeraaald!' squealed Delphina excitedly. 'I can't wait for our fitting. Aren't you excited?'

'Erm,' I said, not wanting to hurt her feelings. 'I suppose so.'

Delphina, Mum, and I swam over to where Auster was trying on headdresses. They were all very regal looking.

'The bigger the better, I say!' he declared, placing a very large, very ornate-looking headdress on top of his head. It was dripping with gold coins and gems that tinkled when he moved.

'What do you think?' he asked, turning towards us. Delphina clasped her hands together, grinning.

'I love it, Dad! I want one just as big and fancy!'

I watched as Mum and Delphina had fun trying on lots of different styles. There were so many to choose from—twirly and swirly, ritzy and pearly. They all looked very . . . *royal*. And totally not *me*.

I hugged Inkibelle close and I think I must have hugged her a tiny bit too hard because she suddenly shot out of my arms in a flurry of bubbles, catapulting up onto the shelves above my head.

'Watch out!' Delphina shouted, as a
large headdress fell down from the shelf
above, and landed right on my head!
Inkibelle must have knocked it off!

'Ow!' I cried. I tried to pull the crown
off but the fiddly little jewels kept tangling

in my wavy spiky hair. I pulled harder but
it seemed to just make everything worse.
Every time I managed to get one part of
the crown free, another part got stuck!

'Oh dear, let me help,' said Madame
Cowrie, swimming towards me with a large
pair of shiny silver scissors.

I stared at her in horror.

'You can't cut my
hair!' I gasped.

'I'm afraid I'll have
to snip a *few* little bits
off,' replied Madame
Cowrie. 'But don't worry.
I'll only cut what's
absolutely *necessary*. No

one will notice with your hairstyle under the headdress anyway!'

Suddenly, I was surrounded by Mum, Auster, and Delphina, all watching Madame Cowrie snip, snip with her scissors. I felt my cheeks blush and eventually the headdress was free.

'There!' said Mum. 'No one will even notice your hair!'

I swam towards the centre of the room, keeping well away from the shelves. I could see Inkibelle hiding behind one of the headdresses with a guilty expression on her face.

'Can we get on with choosing our headdresses now?' said Delphina.

'Yes!' said Mum excitedly, as she placed an extremely pretty and delicate crown upon her head. 'Which one will you choose, Emerald?'

I looked around Madame Cowrie's shop. Pearls, jewels, and sea-glass winked down at me from every shelf, but I just couldn't imagine myself wearing any of it.

'I don't think there's anything really in my style,' I said.

'Oh, of course there is!' replied Mum, swiftly.

'Look at *meee*!' shouted Delphina as she whirled round the shop, wearing the biggest, most majestic headdress she could find. Auster took her hands and they spun together in the water, little bubbles twirling

up towards the octopus-shaped chandelier.

I watched them dance, feeling like there

was a wriggly octopus inside *me*.

'Do you need some help, Emerald?' asked Auster, swimming over with Delphina.

'How about this one?' she asked, picking up a large silver headdress with stars all over it. It still didn't feel as though it was quite me but I had to admit that it was pretty. And I could tell that Delphina was trying to be helpful.

'That one will be fine,' I said, pasting a smile onto my face. 'Thank you, Delphina.'

Chapter THREE

The following evening we had a rehearsal
for the Ocean Parade. The royal carriage
pulled up outside the palace and we
all swam out to admire it. It was very
beautiful—round like a giant silver
bubble, and decorated all over with
swirls, twirls, and jewels. Six beautiful
dolphins were harnessed to the front of

the carriage, looking very regal.

'I love dolphins!' exclaimed Delphina, putting out her hand to pat one of them on the snout. The dolphin squeaked happily.

'Right!' said Auster. 'Everyone get inside the carriage! The dolphins will pull it around the palace gardens and we will practise our waving technique. The Ocean Parade is only two days away!'

He swam into the carriage and sat down on one of the squashy sea-sponge seats. Mum and Delphina followed with me at the back, and Inkibelle squiggling along behind me. I sat down on the seat next to one of the large, open windows.

There was nowhere to hide—*everyone* would be able to see in as we passed!

'Be careful, Emerald!' said Mum, as I accidentally knocked my headdress into her delicate one. A single pearl came floating off her headdress, and landed in her lap.

'Oops, sorry,' I said.

'No worries, Emerald, I'm sure it can be mended before the parade.' Mum smiled at me but I felt bad. I knew how excited Mum was about the headdress she had chosen.

There was a sudden jerk and the carriage started to float through the palace gardens, pulled along by the dolphins. We passed tall seaweed fronds in all the colours of the rainbow. Colourful fish darted about alongside the carriage. They were pretty to look at but I couldn't help remembering that the day after tomorrow it wouldn't just be fish that I would be seeing outside the carriage window.

It would be faces. Hundreds and hundreds of them! Staring at me, wearing my big silver *princessy* headdress.

'We wave like this,' said Auster, showing me how to swish my hands through the water in a regal way.

'And we smile,' he added. 'Don't forget to smile!'

Mum and Delphina waved and smiled, beaming out of the carriage windows at the fish. I tried to do the same.

'Maybe a little more enthusiastically,

Emerald,' said Auster,
kindly.

I waved my
hand faster and harder,
accidentally bopping
Inkibelle so that she swooshed through
the water, leaving a dark ink cloud
behind her that sank down into the
sea-sponge seats.

'Maybe just wave a bit slower,'
coached Mum, sounding a little worried
as she glanced at the ink-stained seat.
'And perhaps you should leave Inkibelle at
home for the parade?'

'No!' I gasped.

I stopped waving for a moment,

feeling my heart beating hard in my chest. I was starting to feel very uncomfortable indeed. Inkibelle came everywhere with me. It wouldn't be fair to leave her at home! I looked down at my hands. First I wasn't waving enough and then I was waving too much—this would never do—I would never be able to look or act like a proper princess!

'Are you all right, Emerald?' asked Mum, putting her hand on my tail.

'I'm fine,' I said.

But I wasn't fine. I didn't feel very princessy at all. I imagined merpeople lining the parade and saying, *What in the name of glimmering gills is that mermaid doing in the royal carriage?'*

'I have to go to the bathroom,' I said,
but then I scooted out of the carriage so
fast that my tail got caught in the door.

'OUCH!' I yelled. I tugged my tail
free and tumbled over into a huge clump
of seaweed nearby. The giant, slimy
fronds waved about, encircling me.
It felt like being wrapped up by a squid.

A big, cold, slimy squid!

'Halt the carriage!' yelled Auster.

I looked up and saw Mum, Auster, and Delphina staring down at me from the carriage window.

'Let me help you,' said Auster, opening the carriage door.

'No!' I shouted, hurriedly unpeeling the seaweed fronds from where they were curled around my body. I just wanted to be alone, in a place where I could be myself and not make any more mistakes.

I swam as fast as I could back into the palace and up to my room. I took off my headdress and threw it on the bed, staring crossly at it. I thought of Mum, Auster, and Delphina all looking so perfect and doing the wave properly and not falling over. I just didn't fit in!

I looked over at my little suitcase. Perhaps I should go and stay at Dad's house just until the Ocean Parade was over. He was away on holiday until next week but that was OK because I wanted to be completely *alone.*

I began to throwing things into my suitcase. Some clothes, my jewellery, my favourite black tiara, my clamshell alarm clock, and Inkibelle's bow.

I was slamming the suitcase shut when there was a knock on the door.

'Emerald?' called Auster. 'Emerald, can I come in?'

I stared at my suitcase and hurriedly shoved it under my duvet.

'Come in,' I said.

'Are you all right, Emerald?' Auster asked, swimming into my room.

'Um . . .' I mumbled, looking into my lap.

'I just wanted to check that everything is OK.'

Auster tentatively sat down next to me on my bed, right on top of my suitcase. Uh-oh . . .

'Ooh!' he said, jumping up and rubbing his tail. 'Your mattress isn't very comfortable!'

He whisked my duvet off and saw my suitcase. Auster frowned, but didn't say anything. Instead, he sat back down *next* to the suitcase this time, and looked thoughtfully around my room.

'You know,' he said, 'I was very nervous the first time I took part in the Ocean Parade. I was worried I wouldn't get the waving right. My hand felt like a wobbly jellyfish!'

I couldn't help smiling a little bit. The idea of Auster with a jellyfish for a hand was funny!

'My father gave me some good advice,' said Auster. 'He told me to just be myself! All you can do is be yourself, Emerald. I'm sorry if we made you feel as though you had to act a certain way. There's absolutely no point in pretending you're someone you're not.'

I looked down at my lap and fidgeted with my hands.

'But I don't feel princessy at all!' I whispered.

'Being a princess is whatever *you* make it,' said Auster. 'You are who you are and becoming a princess shouldn't change that. I *want* you to be yourself!'

'But what if I decide I don't want to be in the parade at all?'

'It's important to me that you feel comfortable, Emerald,' Auster said, 'and I certainly don't want to make you do anything you don't want to do. Maybe sleep on it and see how you feel in the morning?'

I nodded. That was fair.

'OK,' I agreed.

I felt much better after my chat with Auster. He had pretty much said that I didn't have to go in the carriage if I didn't want to, so I decided that I wouldn't!

I put my suitcase away and snuggled under the covers with Inkibelle, feeling pleased. But as I drifted off to sleep, I began to feel a little uneasy. Something was nagging at me. Was there a way to ride in the royal carriage *and* be myself at the same time?

Chapter FOUR

I woke up the next morning with a plan. The Ocean Parade was tomorrow so I didn't have much time!

I swooshed out of bed in a flurry of bubbles and swam down to the great dining hall. 'Mum!' I said excitedly. 'Please can I go over to Oceana's house after school today? Please, please, please!'

Mum blinked in surprise.

'Well, good morning to you too, Emerald!' she said. 'Erm, I don't know about you going to a friend's house *this* evening. It's the Ocean Parade tomorrow. Whether you're coming in the carriage with us or not, you need to be well-rested tonight.'

She smiled at me but I could see that she looked a little worried.

'Pleeeeease!' I begged. 'It's really important!'

'Well all right,' she said. 'But don't be home too late.'

As soon as I got to school, I found Oceana and asked if I could come over to her house at the end of the day.

'Of course!' she replied. 'Shall we ask the others too? Do you want to play catch the bubble? We never ended up playing it the other day.'

'Can it be just us?' I asked. 'There's something else I want to do. You're so good at making things that I was hoping you could help me with something special.'

'Ooh,' she said, intrigued. 'I'd love to!'

After school finished, Oceana and I swam over to her house, which is near my dad's at the other side of Scallop City. She lives

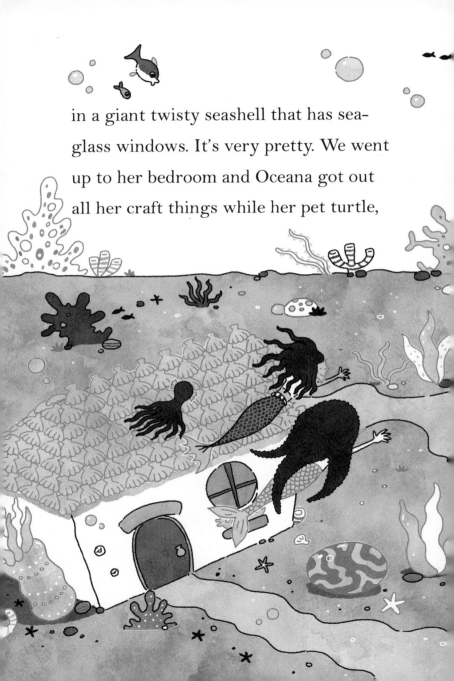

in a giant twisty seashell that has sea-
glass windows. It's very pretty. We went
up to her bedroom and Oceana got out
all her craft things while her pet turtle,

Cleo, played nearby with Inkibelle. There was so much stuff! Beads, buttons, fabric, sequins, and shells. We could create anything we wanted!

'What exactly is it that you want to make?' asked Oceana.

'A headdress,' I replied. 'I think I need to make something that makes me feel more . . . like me!'

'That's a good idea!' Oceana said. 'How about something black, green, and sparkly then? Maybe with an octopus on it like Inkibelle! A sequinned octopus!'

'An octopus!' I said, feeling excited.
Oceana always has the best ideas!

'It could have green crystals all over
its tentacles,' I added. 'To be like emeralds.
Like my name! And I could have some see-
through black fabric coming from my top

that will float about in the water. Ooh, and I could paint my nails black to match!'

'It would really suit you,' said Oceana.

I paused for a moment.

Would wearing an octopus on my head be a bit too . . . different? It would look nothing like my mum's headdress, or Delphina's or Auster's. It might make me stand out even more and I was already worried about merpeople gawping at me. Surely I didn't want to give them *more* to gawp at.

'I suppose it doesn't sound very *princessy* though,' I said.

'I don't think we should worry about that. Let's just make something you love,' said Oceana.

I closed my eyes and imagined myself sitting with my family, wearing my octopus headdress. And it made me feel . . . good!

Suddenly, I felt inspired and sparkly. And fizzy with excitement! I remembered what Auster said about how there was no point in pretending you're someone you're not.

'OK,' I said, glancing at the clock.

'We had better get started!'

★ ★ ★

I arrived back at the palace that evening

feeling tired but excited. Under my arm

I carried a large box with my new

headdress inside.

'What's in the box?' asked Mum

when I came through the door.

'You'll see tomorrow!' I replied.

'Have you decided whether you're coming in the royal carriage tomorrow?' asked Auster.

'I have,' I said. 'And I've decided that I will!'

Mum beamed.

'But . . .' I continued, 'I'm going to be wearing something a bit different and I'd like you to trust me.'

'Trust you, eh?' said Auster, raising his eyebrows. Then he smiled, a big happy grin. 'That's wonderful news, Emerald. We'll look forward to having you in the carriage with us tomorrow.'

Chapter FIVE

I woke up early on the day of the Ocean
Parade—there was so much to do! I got up
and had breakfast with my family and then
swished back up to my room to get ready.
I still felt nervous about going in the
carriage with everyone staring at me, but
now those feelings of nerves were mixed
with excitement too.

When I was ready, I swam downstairs to meet Mum, Auster, and Delphina. They were all floating by the great front doors of the palace waiting for me.

When I appeared, their mouths dropped open in amazement. I was wearing my new headdress—a dark green sequinned octopus that curled around my head with tentacle suckers made from emerald-like crystals. I had painted my nails black and dark starry fabric billowed and glittered all around me. Inkibelle floated nearby, a sequinned emerald-coloured bow on her head.

'Wow!' said Mum. 'You look . . .'

'Fabulous!' yelled Delphina. 'Spellbinding!'

'Erm . . . different,' said Auster, but his eyes were twinkling. 'I see you took my advice on board?'

I nodded.

'I was thinking about what you said and I realized that I would feel so much more confident sitting in the carriage if I felt more like myself. Even if it does make me stand out.'

'Well, I think you look perfectly, magically, *you!*' Auster grinned.

'Yes,' agreed Mum, smiling. 'You're very talented to have made such a beautiful, intricate and *quirky* headdress.

How did you do it?'

'It was all thanks to Oceana!'
I replied. 'And you all look amazing too!'
I meant it. Mum looked sparkling
and regal in her pearly tiara.
Auster looked impressive in
his huge gold headdress
and Delphina looked
charming in all her
princessy sparkle.

'Let's go!' said
King Auster.

I felt the nerves
squiggle around inside
me again as Auster
opened the great front

doors of the palace and led us outside. The carriage was waiting—shimmering and shining in the rays of magical sea light. We all got in and I shuffled up next to the window with Inkibelle on my lap. Outside the palace gates I could see crowds of merpeople, waiting expectantly. I took a deep breath and my mum gave my hand a squeeze.

The dolphins set off and the carriage began to float towards the palace gates, heading out into Scallop City. Everywhere I looked there were merpeople dressed in their sparkling best. Beads, jewels, pearls, shells, and glitter twinkled back at me from every direction. I looked out for my friends and waved out of the window. It wasn't quite a royal wave like Auster's—it was my version instead! I smiled at the crowd and my smile felt real! I was so happy to be in the royal carriage with Mum, Auster, and Delphina.

What's more, I realized that *no one* was gawping. Not in the way I had imagined. I felt a bit silly for thinking that everyone would be so concerned with the way *I* looked. The crowd was a sparkling array of different outfits, styles, and fashions.

I loved it all!

The carriage glided through the water along the streets of Scallop City. Music was playing and merpeople were dancing. The atmosphere was electric! I couldn't help jiggling in my seat too, and Inkibelle began to bop her little tentacles about.

Suddenly, I spotted my friends. They were floating in a little group outside Eel's Emporium. Marina was wearing the beautiful outfit that Oceana had designed for her, and Oceana looked enchanting in a sheer turquoise cloak *covered* in sequin spangles. When they saw me they waved and waved! I waved back excitedly.

'Auster,' I said suddenly. 'Can we stop the carriage? Please?'

Auster hesitated for a moment, but then he nodded.

'I don't see why not,' he said. Auster stuck his head out of the window to call for the dolphins to stop swimming. I swished off my seat and opened the carriage door, swimming out. The merpeople around us gasped. I swam over to my friends and gave them a huge hug.

'Auster!' I shouted. 'Come and meet Oceana. She's the mermaid who made my headdress!'

I pushed Oceana to the front of the crowd. Auster swam out of the carriage, towards us. He looked impressed.

'It's a pleasure to meet you, Oceana,' he said. 'Emerald's headdress is incredible!'

Oceana looked embarrassed but very pleased.

'Thank you,' she whispered. 'But it was nothing really . . .'

'It wasn't *nothing*,' said Auster. 'It was very kind of you to help your friend. I know it means a lot to Emerald.'

'It does,' I agreed, happily.

'Would you like to ride the rest of the way in the carriage with us?' asked Auster.

Oceana's eyes grew as big and round as jellyfish.

'Me?!' she squeaked.

'Yes!' I said, my heart exploding with happiness. There was only one thing better than riding in the royal carriage wearing my octopus headdress, and that was riding in the carriage wearing my octopus headdress with my friend by my side! I took Oceana's hand and dragged her towards the carriage. We wriggled in together and she sat down beside me on the seat, fidgeting.

Delphina was excited to have another mermaid in the carriage with us too, and we all sat there giggling and laughing while Auster and Mum shook the hands of all the merpeople in the crowd nearby. Then they both returned to the carriage and we set off again. I waved and waved, until my hand felt like it might drop off!

The carriage swept on through the parade until finally we reached the end of our journey back at the palace, where lots of fancy food stalls had been set up. We swam out of the carriage to enjoy the celebrations. Auster swished straight over to a food stall and handed a seafood skewer to each of us.

'Mmm!' said Delphina.

'It's nice,' said Oceana. But in my ear she whispered, 'Not *quite* as nice as the coral floss and sea ices in the centre of Scallop City though!'

'True!' I agreed. 'But the thing is, I think we are supposed to stay in the palace grounds now that the parade is over.'

I felt a bit disappointed. It would be fun to find Marina, Finn, and Aqua.

'It *did* look fun down in the centre of Scallop City,' Delphina said. 'But we can have fun here too! I know all the best food stalls and look, there's some fish balloons!'

I looked over to where some beautiful balloons were bobbing in the water, all with rainbow shimmery scales.

'I'll get one for you!' said Delphina kindly. She whooshed over to the balloon stall just as Auster came swimming over with some delicious sweet seaberry smoothies. A moment later, Delphina swam back with a balloon trailing behind her, and handed it to me.

'Oh, that's pretty!' Oceana sighed as we both gazed at it for a moment. Then a band started to play and Oceana and I decided to have a dance, watching the way the balloon bobbed and glinted in the sea light. As we were twizzling, twirling, and loop the looping, I saw Delphina swim up to Mum and Auster and say something to them. A few minutes later they all came swimming over.

94

'Delphina says that the three of you would like to go into the centre of Scallop City?' Auster said.

'Oh um . . .' I began.

'I'd *really* like to go!' said Delphina, giving Mum and Auster her most charming smile. 'I saw they had coral floss and sea ices when we went past in the carriage!'

I held my breath, waiting to see what they would say.

'I'll tell you what,' Auster said. 'Why don't we *all* go!'

We climbed back into the carriage and the dolphins pulled us back through the streets of Scallop City, towards the

centre, where
Oceana and
I spotted our
friends. They were
taking it in turns to
balance on manta rays,
using them to whizz through the water.
Finn was whooping with delight as he
swooshed up, down, and all around,
holding tightly onto the reins.

'Ooh!' said
Delphina. 'I'd like
a go on a
manta ray!'

'Me too!'
said Oceana.

'Me too!'
said Auster and
I turned to him
in surprise.

'I used to be very
good at manta ray gliding when I was a
young merboy,' he said. 'I'll have to show
you all!'

We swam out of the carriage and
over to my friends who seemed surprised
to see us.

'We didn't think you'd be back!' said
Aqua.

'I'm glad you made it though,'
grinned Marina. She had a crown of sea
flowers on her head and the petals waved

97

gently in the underwater current.

I smiled back at her. My heart felt full.

We all watched Auster have a go
on a manta ray, holding tightly onto
the reins and whizzing backwards
and forwards.

'Oops!' he said, as he fell off it for
the hundredth time. I think he might
have been telling a fib about being
good at it as a merboy! I saw Mum roll
her eyes, fondly.

There was a crowd gathered
around us now. Everyone was laughing

as they watched the king play around
on the manta ray and he looked like he
was having the best time ever.
I suddenly realized that, just like
me, Auster didn't always look or act
exactly like a royal either.

'That was fun!' Auster whooped when he finally finished manta ray gliding. 'Thank you for suggesting we come here, Delphina and Emerald!' His headdress was wonky and his hair was all messed up, but he didn't seem to mind. 'What shall we do now?'

'Get coral floss and sea ices?' said Delphina hopefully.

'Your wish is my command!' replied Auster. 'But where do we get that from?'

'I'll show you!' offered Oceana.

We all followed her across the crowded square to a food stall and chose our flavour of coral floss and sea ice. I went for purple seaberry! Then we sat down to eat them. Inkibelle kept poking out her tentacle to steal little bits!

'Delicious!' said Auster, smacking his lips. 'Do you know, I have never had a sea ice before.'

'Really?!' said Mum in surprise. 'Maybe we ought to come out into Scallop City more often!'

'I'd love that,' said Auster. 'You and Emerald can show me all the best places to eat.'

I smiled. I couldn't help it. I felt like I was overflowing with happiness! It was so nice to just sit here, tail to tail with all my friends, Mum, Delphina, and Auster, listening to music, eating sea ices, laughing and feeling like *myself*. This year's parade was turning out to be just as good as last year's parade . . .

No, actually . . .

It was *better*!

Quiz

Which merperson are you?
Take the quiz to find out!

**1. You are going to the Ocean Parade!
How would you like to take part?**

A. I would be riding in the royal carriage,
waving out of the window at my friends.

B. I would rather be watching the parade with
all my friends and a big stick of coral floss.

C. I would be skating alongside the royal carriage
on my manta ray!

2. What do you like to do in your spare time?

A. Drawing and making things
at home.

B. Playing with my pets or
spending time with animals.

C. Skateboarding in the park.

3. If a friend was in need, what would you do?

A. Ask if they would like to hang out and
do something I know they enjoy.

B. Ask if they were OK.
A problem shared is a problem halved.

C. Invite them to play a game of rounders with a
group of friends, to cheer them up.

Results

Mostly As

You are a creative super star just like Oceana! You love using
your imagination to create amazing pieces of art. You're a
great friend who is kind and empathetic.

Mostly Bs

You are a natural around animals and your friends love spending
time with you just like Emerald. You are fun, funny and kind.

Mostly Cs

You are bursting with energy and your enthusiasm is
infectious just like Finn! You love playing with your friends
and using all that energy to spread a bit of happiness
everywhere you go.

Fruit skewers

There's lots of yummy food at the Ocean Parade, including Delphina's favourite, seafood skewers. If seafood isn't your thing, here's how you can make fruit skewers at home.

What you will need:

★ Some wooden kebab skewers

★ A knife

★ A grown up to help

Method:

1. Cut and peel your fruit into tasty bite-sized morsels.

2. Push them on to the kebab stick in an order of your choice.

3. Enjoy!

How to make your very own headdress

Emerald and Oceana made a fabulous headdress that was totally, uniquely perfect for Emerald. Why don't you think about all the things you love, and make a totally unique headdress of your own?

What you will need:

★ Coloured paper

★ Scissors

★ Hole punch

★ Ribbon

★ Plastic gems, sequins, or anything else you can think of to decorate your headdress.

★ PVA glue

Method:

1. Cut out a headband shape from the coloured paper.

2. Punch a hole in both ends of your headband shape.

3. Thread a ribbon through each hole and tie a knot in the end to secure it.

4. Decorate your headdress.

Harriet Muncaster, that's me! I'm the author and illustrator of the Isadora Moon, Mirabelle, and Emerald books. I love anything teeny tiny, anything starry, and everything glittery.

To visit
Harriet Muncaster's
website, visit
harrietmuncaster.co.uk

ISADORA · MOON

ISADORA · MOON
Goes to School

Half vampire, half fairy, totally unique!
Harriet Muncaster

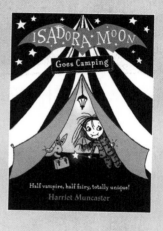

ISADORA · MOON
Goes Camping

Half vampire, half fairy, totally unique!
Harriet Muncaster

ISADORA · MOON
Has a Birthday

Half vampire, half fairy, totally unique!
Harriet Muncaster

ISADORA · MOON
Goes to the Ballet

Half vampire, half fairy, totally unique!
Harriet Muncaster

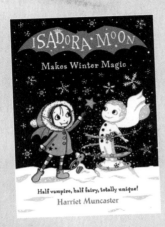

ISADORA MOON

Makes Winter Magic

Half vampire, half fairy, totally unique!

Harriet Muncaster

ISADORA MOON

Goes to the Fair

Half vampire, half fairy, totally unique!

Harriet Muncaster

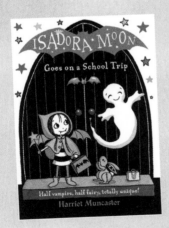

ISADORA MOON

Goes on a School Trip

Half vampire, half fairy, totally unique!

Harriet Muncaster

ISADORA MOON

Gets in Trouble

Half vampire, half fairy, totally unique!

Harriet Muncaster

ISADORA MOON

Has a Sleepover

Half vampire, half fairy, totally unique!
Harriet Muncaster

ISADORA MOON

Puts on a Show

Half vampire, half fairy, totally unique!
Harriet Muncaster

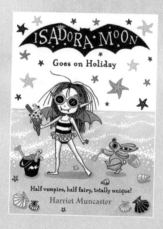

ISADORA MOON

Goes on Holiday

Half vampire, half fairy, totally unique!
Harriet Muncaster

ISADORA MOON

Goes to a Wedding

Half vampire, half fairy, totally unique!
Harriet Muncaster

ISADORA MOON
Meets the Tooth Fairy

Half vampire, half fairy, totally unique!
Harriet Muncaster

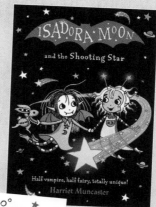

ISADORA MOON
and the Shooting Star

Half vampire, half fairy, totally unique!
Harriet Muncaster

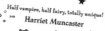

ISADORA MOON
Under the Sea

Plus Isadorable activities!

Half vampire, half fairy, totally unique!
Harriet Muncaster

ISADORA MOON
Gets the Magic Pox

Half vampire, half fairy, totally unique!
Harriet Muncaster

ISADORA MOON
and the New Girl

Half vampire, half fairy, totally unique!
Harriet Muncaster

MIRABELLE

From the world of ISADORA MOON

MIRABELLE
Gets up to Mischief

Half witch, half fairy, totally naughty!
Harriet Muncaster

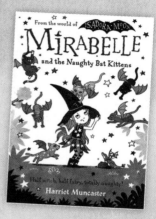

From the world of ISADORA MOON

MIRABELLE
and the Naughty Bat Kittens

Half witch, half fairy, totally naughty!
Harriet Muncaster

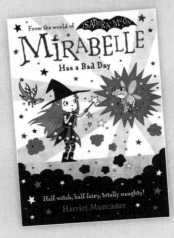

From the world of ISADORA MOON

MIRABELLE
Has a Bad Day

Half witch, half fairy, totally naughty!
Harriet Muncaster

From the world of ISADORA MOON

MIRABELLE
Breaks the Rules

Half witch, half fairy, totally naughty!

Harriet Muncaster

From the world of ISADORA MOON

MIRABELLE
in Double Trouble

Half witch, half fairy, totally naughty!

Harriet Muncaster

From the world of ISADORA MOON

MIRABELLE
Takes Charge

Half witch, half fairy, totally naughty!

Harriet Muncaster

From the world of ISADORA MOON

MIRABELLE
and the Magical Mayhem

Half witch, half fairy, totally naughty!

Harriet Muncaster

Love Emerald?
Why not try these too...

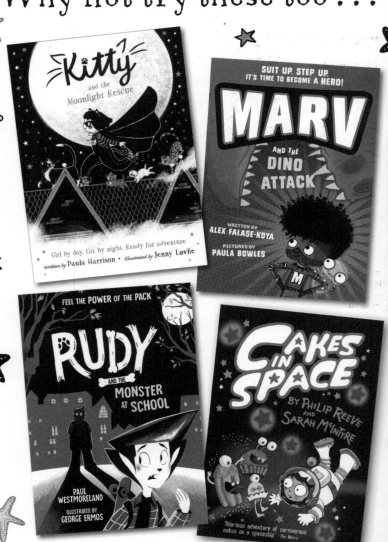